ANATOMY COURSES

PRAISE FOR BLAKE BUTLER

"An endlessly surprising, funny, and subversive writer."
—*Publishers Weekly*

"If the distortion and feedback of Butler's intense riffing is too loud, you may very well be too boring."
—*Globe and Mail (Toronto)*

"Try Blake on. Lace him up. Wear him around your neck in wreaths."
—*Vice*

"If there's a more thoroughly brilliant and exciting new writer than Blake Butler . . . well, there just isn't."
—**Dennis Cooper**

PRAISE FOR SEAN KILPATRICK

"This is a book you need. Language reset. Guidebook."
—**HTML GIANT** on Sean Kilpatrick's *fuckscapes*

"The violent, sexual zone of television and entertainment is made to saturate that safe-haven, the American Family. The result is a zone of violent ambience, a 'fuckscape': where every object or word can be made to do horrific acts. As when torturers use banal objects on their victims, it is the most banal objects that become the most horrific (and hilarious) in Sean Kilpatrick's brilliant first book."
—**Johannes Goransson** on *fuckscapes*

"Here is your I.V. drip of sphinx's blood."
—**CA Conrad**

A Lazy Fascist original

Lazy Fascist Press
An imprint of Eraserhead Press
205 NE Bryant Street
Portland, OR 97211

Interior design by Cameron Pierce

An excerpt from *Anatomy Courses* first appeared in *Caketrain*.

ISBN: 978-1-62105-018-6

Printed in the USA.

ANATOMY COURSES

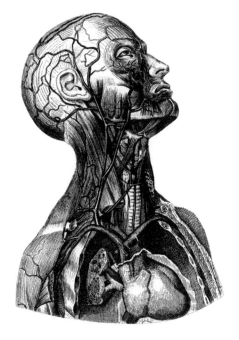

BLAKE BUTLER
SEAN KILPATRICK

LAZY FASCIST PRESS
PORTLAND, OREGON

The device could not control my anger. I felt thirsty to throw up.
I bit my eyelids, shitting yearlings. In the cornea, the blood.

Among the antique air our skins were leakage. Our house gyrated
unasked speech, squirting peals from glue-shaped daughters we'd
surrendered. Bright days made crystal bodies of the sound inside
us and spread them through anywhere we slept: massive ash
closets stuffed with hungry sons and wives sporting Daewoo; fat
phantom-actors who loved this land. I'd hid the father's evening
costume in every flame again.

Sourceless throblight through my private window made the
room tonight decide on *gone*.

I held my glee. My hurting anus helmet. Gold robes of sweat
and hussy cake dumped from the date. I scrunched inside
the coronation mattress, asking where *where* was. My ovum
bubbled. I spread my holes an arm-width each, saying pristine
in the accent of the snitch: *our lord is both our lesion and our lung*.

Sweet cream erupted from my slits: in slaving whips and older hours already lard for our Alzheimer's. The father's tongues had reamed in me another child. A child of leather, also preggers, unglowing limbs of gas that rose and fell and rose again, and killed again and filled my lengths and made me simple. I'd freely sold our sorrowsleep for ass and Pablum.

Between such shapes my colors gored. *Where had I been since you were in here*, I asked each passage. *What fields of you where all around me days rained face.* I felt our generation bloat and kneel inside my pork seeking its dogdoor. Beyond the door, a decade's wait unto forgetting—dressed now in the down of breath of dying hitmen kissed upon my muff in christened glyphs, and every hour so Corroder. The mother-graft of me grew underneath us modern—*and into you again, sewn for no mourning.* Our herpes moan gushed up a high and scrying wind.

Full moan for throblight. I milk myself alive. Pap smears anoint me. My area code is SIKE.

I lugged the father's ringworm. Under his crouton, prolapsed juggle, gagging for subpoenas, ground in weave, chromosome fed, the device sagging. I cuddled the father's fleas, webbing my switch, jinxed the whorl: *Coin that cootie.* Our lipping bacne through rooms askance. Birthcurd delivery, I hutted so veldt. The father taste-tested how hung.

Pray for balloons during the father's placenta. Jump the kiss right out of his flay. How he was born made a toy of the ghetto. Such skinny lotions douse his sway. **Howdy ya'll.**

The mother flaring wrinkles, pressing cysts inside, huffing cilia, tomahawked my dung across her woof. She spoke for Iraq, plucking her frown. She screened my whole peepshow. I tapped her ribs yellow, ballad of collapsed lung, dangling from what was.

Gimmie boo boo honey. Gimmie change for whitey's dump. Gimmie clothes-pinned poots the mother memorized as me. The fat child gleaming, needstunk, yikes and whim.

Though I swallowed exits in the womb.

The hallway lurched in vision, smeared the smears of any I. Our lapse-gunk gushed from keyholes in the night where dark had curled to rim itself. Even the NBA today felt retro-obese and dismissive. Giddy walls of bulging fist-light whimpered always. Bliss curtains in the downstairs caught our blood tides, where my last son sneezed storks and ugly-fits. Mud above us. Black above that. We halving *having* into *ha*. The cradle burrowed in our lungs dialing the landlord to bring trash bags full of soot that we could be.

My piglet rent was late, but I'd slayed Seagram's and my new milking gown got nice. With one spurt we'd found the fountain in the crawdad-buried Mall of Steers, where drunk once on blowtorch fuel and TV denim the father'd shrunk his life in mind into a coin—*this coin in the future bought the lambskin ceiling with matching cocoon jumpsuits for our whole home + all our guns.*

Fatboyed I hid up in the thinnest dressing room behind the

women's want-pit and watched them snarfing Hank the Fifth. Their nipples clammed a miming anthem. It got me smashed and held my hands. I was a child in here. I was cheerleaders. But I wanted even better. I gross-forced my best hand where I was thickest—fully crammed once again into the dry vibrating eye of my huge bud. I pulled and pulled—popping, green steam, and hiccups—a wider force like birds of meth—then something in me too was also pulling. I could not let it go. I felt a strong and high alarm sound flooding where our lungs were. I became glow-choked and unwalled like a church. I could no longer see to what other earths I could conform from that point forward— just this old one smoking blackhole bending in against itself, gaudy forever at your service, juiced on the caulk of human math.

The father's gum grew in me so far I often was the father, the wax lining of his grudge. Whenever enacting the bile duct for his daily birthday, I felt someone in me like him always row—my next boys of his screaming through masks of fish for a pillow made bald with worshipped sod to squirt their eggs against and snack until they had made hands of their own, which made me jelly-spittle all my yellow. I heard me shouting in repetition the only sentence I'd ever heard. This had to quit and had just got numbing. I wanted to go shopping badly at a Sears, or any place that still sold blenders. *What grit was living in me now.* I rubbed my mess off on a Black's cracker and ate it shaking. I called the troops to come escort me to our cell. In the milk of shuttering horizons: a giddy hog without a shape.

I shoved my new boy-nub into the lamp to give us light for

sleeping. Everyday hid everyday. In the eastern-facing window, the newly limbless undressed women sung stuck scraping pigskin off their eyes.

We would profit stool the father jiggled. Goiters his wives smoked by news, a motor-pile of children their laundry did, stretching macular. Crisp and Christly buckets tingled our gender.

Moist wool inside our clap, husky periods, formed the spine of neighborhoods chugging into dial, a concert scabbing matter. We clicked our teeth on hurt airs. Gonging thigh-crud advertisements.

I knitted the albino further fracture, diving hetero from her pouch. We counseled our spots.

Portioning, my valves zoomed the father frottage, sippy cup colostomy. I timed his honey. Stapled his will. The sheets channeled vivacious grime. A lot of dopamine nestled in there. A lot of molestation borrowed from other families caught the linen.

Freebasing the mother's chamber pot, all I saw was syrup. Her menopause sequined my asthma. I became her neutered nurse and worshipped hornets.

We sold ourselves without knowing.

We bitty tamed, sizzled iffy, worshipping furnaces. In each basement the father piloting my tits so we could stand. We never rose sans burn marks. Being burnt was finally us.

Behind the father in the kitchen. He sucked our doubled infant's chubs. His nostrils poured police scent. Porkrind Child music gifting rings upon my fingers. Teething teeth on adult molars. Hexagonal keyholes in my cummy coil network.

Clean gobbled, the infant was returned to its indention behind the erased painting of my body teaching our family pet to mate with gravel. It was the most fulfilling work I'd done since Golden Corral closed. I could hear the babe's limbs through the drywall playing *Where's the Curl?* with his screwdriver. So cute I wanted mutton up my sleep zone.

The father would not comply. Alone with no butts but mine again he sobbed into the sockets, shorting sections of the cul-de-sac our ideal dim. I put my thumb against his father skull-sac, the soft spot he'd never healed from endless ramming. I worked my thumb in and we grew gold. Prayed in rhythm with the invocation Braille he'd risen. The Down's became a gift. The father could no longer fully stand—his erection in the sentence.

His book, a godded pup tent, kissed the world.

With each blink we changed another letter until the woman in me also blinked. The sound confessor stood up all around us, ox and model, *and what crumbs fell from his lap.* Wedding cake of my pimp, mad Dr. Rimmon, with the organ of Ronove [*behind all veils*]. I mommy-walked until my scrotum inhaled in my bush meat and sprayed me with mace. I became interested in typing to prisoners. My spore erupting weekends in the mists of dream vacation with the father up-necked in every burnt skin bar.

Again, my anger stoked me open—cored with massive maggots in black mayo, slung from cold trombones.

I broke each leg to process distance. The hallway administering bed time stories wrapped in chemotherapy. I weaned my rashes. Tricked out my water by the fireplace. The lipids of my bladder shone.

The device gasconaded trigonometry, PA system scraggle. Cafeterias vended no scalp by hours of the tinier version of us mechanized within us.

We malted our dollars to swoon.

I slept in a newspaper wide enough to crown my wave. A microphone shitted sons from the knotted tunnel of a senator's hysterectomy. The father singed his clue.

Our neighbors brought the cuticle. Creamed wires to scrub spaces through our wish. The father pulled a slow fracture in their baby. We clapped around the wound. We passed its shavings back and forth in a campy bib. The father spray-painted the little groin black so he could pop and suck without regretting his own genetics.

The father's mind inside the neighbor toddler, an altar wet with text: *No one is here and here is pleasure. A t-shirt for your aphid-ate Delete Me costume.*

The toddler's neighbor's frottage rattled open. In the greaseflesh there was my biggest 4D ego drawing dungeons. Our lobotomy was handy. Cunt comedian. Come rain.

The father spent the next decade stitched into the underbelly of all laughter, sucking the pulp out of a picture of the glitched child I'd most wanted in me always and could not phrase. The one vein in his imagination's microscopic cock invested in a very special fern. I was that fern and always will be.

The father came back out into the backyard where his double had chewed a nation in our sand. The swingset hung with chocolate swastika-kissed anvils, seats grafted fat with toddler head all pushed from me. 17,000 reconstructed negroids watched from the sidelines behind authenticated diamond shades of sun. The father gurfed and snurred and spurted up a mind-sized wad of Best Buy, unchewed from the mother's gums. *The mother in the kitchen with the teacup and saucer giving toasts to Liquid God, downloading handmade prayer rugs from the Burmese sweatshop she'd rented to the bottom half of our whole house—where she still liked most to get reamed while eating: cherry gravy, denim, ice.*

The father went to the window and lifted the neighbor's baby up. He shouted *Loose meat!* at the mother. He tapped and tapped the baby head against the home glass until he'd formed a reason for getting up at all that year. *The baby's forehead smeared goofy in text from next week's New York Times arts section, reviews of vegan cookbooks by LaVey.* The father put the baby downdown in the yard blood. He went into the exploding room instead.

When will the news anchor shit me a perfect night? I heard the baby spoot already.

The father back inside me, dressing in the moss gown of his brides.

Fever skies.

I took the brown mask off the baby. I plugged my skin into the leak. With groan loaned from some summer I threw myself into the tumor, where I'd be quiet for a while.

Some brides peddled oxygen their bygone hymens left. Mucus-centuries whipped forth whole Schlitz, dinging sanctimonious, ton-buttered. I bought a friend sluiced in gulp. Her renouncement fastened hepatitis, diapered, romping about throats. The dark became uterine reject. The home I was killing my way toward.

I shanked bride 101010101000 with Vitamin C. She fiddled her tremors. I had legal rights to all I shook. My labia wings, risen to attack mode by protractor, parted an island through Smuckers. The jags I put. I took my year off nagging holes with metal.

The fathersoda fizzled *sphincter* in faltering designs, in increasingly poor imitation of the rings of his unique sphincter. Balling plastic piled trails we kept secret.

I stopped my fork against prepuce lint haloing the room's changing sun. *I'm fucking mom to show you what folding means*, he said, the baby's split dermis goring his grind, sweat glands burst, clotted in the imposed repetition, new rising bulbs swelling his temperature, his six inches of foreskin tied around the balls, purpled with blood-loss, former throb of the mess fucked around him, his stub continuously ejaculating black water, his gestures larger than he was, the wife he called these organs dropping off the table piecemeal, *like an IRS dreamboat*, he finished, using both hands to stuff back his tongue.

God why does our baby have to be black, the father stuttered, the child half-inside him, half with its head hung on the fainting table. The mother'd milked herself a ghetto clinic into the idgit-light to flex her tong on. *At least how many pussies does it have?*

By now the men from Comcast had wheeled the skin bar against the neighbor's poolhouse's vinyl-siding's smear—pus gray & hung with back knives so splintered at the tips they rubbed a horse into a napkin. The neighbors in their snorkels watched dad's tooter squee in post-ejection sponge. In the shade from the goatskin awning speaking crud I flexed my tongue and thumbed my nut. Still $157 short of blowjob lessons. The mailbox in the morning would splay lice, a shunning rainbow.

Inside our house the hallway shifted upslant toward the Christ-room in such a way and at such angle that it protruded like a lid over the street and the neighboring McDonald's.

I said how many motherfuckin' ooh-zones does the fuckin' pussy baby have? goes Dad. *How many holes?*

Dimes were flying from last Sunday. The matching crotches of our Nation Jammies birthed a 1-800 for getting whapped for free in the grits-kisser. Bean-colored trailers parked the graveyard flat.

In the lapse of several years of the Boxcutter, the ground made booboo yogurt at our knees and ruined my slacks.

A pore is a hole also.

The father went inside a minute and came back out carrying the mother carrying her mother, all three shunts welded into a chandeliering point, adorned on the long end with the brass cockhead Granny had rendered from her visions of ex-husbands. The father's backass shit-satchel fanny pack brimmed behind him in the era, creaming the gears of cameras. The liquid throbber parted the lip folds of our Wheel of Fortune flag, though behind our own glowing cubes cut the whole gum-pink font-index surged through to liquidate the contestants and their birthdates on the invisi-Pixie air. The host in spandex dreampants on his cell phone with my lady reach-around: *Come in Crowley, this is Crowley.*

Crowley, please…

Stop acting like my pussy is an ambulance for the world.

Bigger with fecal incontinence, the mother festered knowledge of cervixes so rubbery, spat tandem flub, more awesome than dribble, could maim surface, pencil-tipping her crimp. Wadding camped between clocks: All families condone slaves, slop a life, she came, a powder. The Salutation Manual stubbed her dog parts.

I hurled receivers up the ache, pancaking her cellulite, and lapped the father's scrota, three-way flounder, going dang. The gang rapes we swam through, pigtailed, bubbling opera, tubular poundage. Luger repeat-firing pistols cautioned our glee. Nubbed the inhabitant day.

Our genitalia-shine waterfalled straight. The father positioned himself in a girl's passing mouth mid-verb and forged sockets. She lost alphabets. The father operated her larynx underhand as the totality of expressions she would pose. Watching her furthered cavity tune some decade.

We corpse about chocolate, banging open slinky-lamps. The room tricked out rotisserie. *No touch is bad.* The glass floor, cum-patterned, creaked a flog through our miles. We tongued the air conditioner for potassium. All his curl just chink spoons. The father cleared me from his fly. *I'll have you fixed*, he moaned. *You did already, boo*, the mother piped up. The father remembered neither doing. He spread scar plaster where my babies weren't. *Looks reputable*, he yawned. His enema splashed cardboard stroller to stroller. He sacrificed his waters.

The mother stood to bump her head against His coffin. Rashed like Nancy, my confessor. I was seeing every inch of light as of my prior lives. The puncture box blanched black. The breath in the box was a machete made of matches.

I cleaved my pussy into ten. The crabs had a decision.

The mother slowdanced through the kitchen with my last precious end-the-baby hanger flexed to ribcage my winter coat—*the coat I wore to prom the year the DJ licked the vinyl, then my hand, and lashed together we watched the men snort baby powder off the popped condoms of our songs. You could count the hard-ons with a mallet.*

Outside her sleep the mother looked so young. I wanted to abort her too.

A slow fist through her sac wall unwrapped the presence of no ancestor in the ground.

Mind-up in mud, the father mattered. The father slit the center of his tongue. He read the invocation rolodex into a mic that wormed his voice back into meat: *Rico the Backfucker, Ham Sandwich, Hardee's employee with reversal scrotum and Jockey endorsement, Mary the Mary, Pockdick Judd.* God could I remember the father's bathwater. Mustard dollop in the Joy. The father in the bathroom mirror on the PA, reading his parasite's revision of *Esther* into the backyard where kids would come to wash their cracks in the dog's dish.

In drumnight the dog would appear before me, curdled, curling up my decoy-privates, but by then I had the world.

The mother came back into the map and bit it raw—we felt new continents of fairy. Her cheek again in jab blood bought forever, wetting egg sacs of our sons' dreamboats. There the father lapped the next eight years using my sissywhipped division of Mind of Hegel. I pissed my wheaties on your birthday, with the candles in my Nancy trough.

Sometimes I say cunt just to say cunt, the father shouted, stalling. His Duck Head shorts in semen tint. He'd wiped his ass on every wedding's diamond. *Today I can't reach through the TV.*

The mother at the front room window speaking Spanish to the weed eater with the Sharpie marker at her forehead and the jack-in-the-box up her behind. *Her fucked-ass big-ass behind,* the father preached, making my thoughts his. He ripped out his bicuspids and threw them at my mind.

The mother with her new mustache, cheek muscles blistering the glass with what little words she knew: *Adios, si, culo, Diablo, Corona, adios.*

The father chiseled my cock from the freezer, crooning: *darn skin ain't no shrine*. The kitchen crusty weep. *Pedro stuck a dildo in my heart*. I sprang, fluting his. A hole chipped perfect blue from piss-colander. The motherjowls' fluent eras. The father rattled my snow between his tooth, trying to drown. He did the saddest beatbox.

The neighbor's child finally grew through her noose. The father stuck a pencil in her belly button, clapped the hem of her dress in the toilet so she couldn't leave. She urinated on her shadow. On her pubis until age reversed, double dare. Her miniscule lobes done volcano, each looping, inoculated, ceramic. Her tunneling cluck.

She tampon'd the whole second grade, spraying her dress with juice boxes. *Fine-tune this dude for slaughter*, the father yelped. *I'm holding up her insides with my cock*, he searched my hand to pat sweat. *Twist them in a question mark, father*, the mother sighed. *The first father of American royalty pulling out. She's hiding some excellent sideburns under there, sirs.* The neighbor girl now sideways postulate foam.

We gave her a slow mastectomy with ice cream. Bored, we upped our sorry. The father baked his genital warts and smeared them into her ground. *I have to go back to the puddle now*, she cried, already within her quarantine. A coma full of snow exploded from the skink.

The bathroom pledging allegiance to carnations vilified by sheen. The tutu markings where my first love opened her bowels and named the universe.

The tubes we used to lift her shed a coloring book mapping all the slush I couldn't lever free, or rip the egg, even with the father's help. I toileted so fast the air became night around us culled home in a micro-evolved box.

Used baby wipes trampoline my composure when I think, I thought.

My thoughts blew blonde from my behind: *when I wake I will have turned to powder*, I was saying, and: *in my slavering, the gong*. My headvoice had my backbone's eject button turned reverse and razed my mind against it in dry reason, made my tummy elevator stay GQ. My whole chest's husk would shift to rooms of anvils. My eggs shat Disney money.

You pour me wine.

All these shopping malls were sweating. My lungs would not fit inside my imitation for all the frosting ditz, the beestings. I had my lips covered in delight loam, my 100,000 glands swoll into a high-dollar handbag marred with crosses, wooed by babies wished in Ambien disease. *By the time they were done removing my left kidney the induction gown would have unraveled, my mother's wet would draw the grub committee, and we would eat.*

I punched myself in the chest until I could feel the lining dying, another form of sleep. Our neighbor's negroids sang Goodnight

Mystery while I mummified my high. My hands jacked off in celebration the glass dong my father had on my fifth birthday hung around my neck, its crystal sperm coils clawing through the flat to scratch against my windpipe. My wish for every pump to be in and around me. My glands gaining 18 pounds in 18 minutes. A need for vomit filled my hands with silver coins. From my back my matching nightmare boner woke the finest of white coats. And the corned beef spritzing through my nostrils, ruining the invocation dinner mints and bib.

You pour me wine.

This chocolate Auschwitz burns my eyes! the father shouted, through a pinhole window in the upstairs. His moustache crashed with urine cake. I could tell he'd been weight-lifting. His lung holds had the quiver. In his hair den, he'd been rebuilding the Holocaust in sweets. Starlite Mints were Jews. Blintz crumbs fashioned bullwhips. My hysterectomy was Rommel. The pamphlets wrote themselves. *My come will not accept the insignia I've provided!* The father went on, choking in his suds. I heard our safety exits crusting over. *I have no passion! The year is lard ass! The steak dinners wake at eight!*

The father cooed inside my wombs, where someone thicker than us filibustered, then appeared.

The father held up 17 colostomy bags abounding his abdomen in perfect imitation of motherfist. The mother emptied each stoma the few instances a day her Alzheimer's circled back long enough to be sanitary. The hardened shit bedecking her walker formed a key she plugged into her children. Her children suckling nightly on the father stomas for a better clean.

The surgical-neat tucks of him slick with our lapping quivered out the undigested snacks he often hid from mother sometimes whole and we made bland faces picking jalapeño pepper from our teeth. The father's diarrhea was our only travel.

The father tongued my sac a hematoma. I was lifted to the ceiling and from there could spill the ponies he mentioned fisting. The carrion next door wiped her tummybulb under the fridge for fake consumption. Thought bubbles over my atrocity. The father bugled in her shallow stank, vortex puppysong. I fussed about her terrarium bowels spruced by hatchlings. My eyes like a second bible punching houses under.

The father unclasped his irrigation valve, peeping lifespans. He once tickled a narcoleptic code on the neighbor's wife. The father's excitement sped the stomas. The bags whispered dust, expellant of the siphon, closer. The father's dowry was just the holocaust. He made a pony of the mother until she remembered everything.

My doubled skin cells spun to stand up, a ladder into the scumming skylid's crease. The CNN horizon formed a prism where honky ballboys were shooting off, their googoo mounds of pregush in dented spheres several times the size of my torso here or yours—*the scored child gum flesh forever sizzled in 1 Corinthians, so slow.* The father's back burped slave lacerations of prismatic VHS scenes where for eons I railed on orange concussions, my panties burned into my skeleton. Underneath, my mental throne, holding the room where you were born, where your mother, as you conformed out, awakened gas ovens in your lungs, the deforming bodies shunted soft into a landfill, gifting you your name, and having so named, opened the cream of you, awoke the mouth in every mouth.

In remembrance, the mother slat her skirt up, shouting lard into the eon's vents. My tits booshed rashy keyholes. Happy.

I had dinner with Ted Bundy seventeen times! the father screamed inside us. His upper lip would not come unstuck, scrunched on Reader's shitty reading-arm, herein appearing through the center of the room. His voice made mashed potatoes lump up in my armpit gymnasium. My nostrils drank us in—first thing I'd ate since Josh. *Ol' Ted sold me a hacksaw and I used it on the bruised lip of my unit. Do you know what I found inside that mess? Laid in the meat there? In the yeast fleas? Do you know what I'd been hiding? The thing inside the thing inside the thing of me?*

The father's Dog Dictionary handwriting on my thorax: "VELPERRUM NOD CONDITION: my definition: *bye*." I erased it with my eye and it became every bed.

Downstairs the mother formed an armchair of her body. There was a ramming in the seat, the seat had held 10,000 asses and would hold 150,000,000,000,000 more. The sweat already ladled in the cushions fed the new child hidden in the mother, veiled in the globular black bulge formed on her left ham locker wrapped inside her large intestines. The mice flesh in the mother's left vagina slowly gorged away by the forming of the new child's hunger. Each time in the chair the mother tried to speak the foot rest sprung and crushed a skull.

I drank a latte with David Berkowitz! The fucking shit was too fucking goddamn hot! My lips made Magic Eye to hide my language. I could not get them open for several years. I threw the burn onto the woman in the trenchcoat behind the counter who had brought her only child to work. The child with its whole head in the whipped cream, snorting. The whole room was snowing. I began to count the tip jar money. David leaned over with my hands full of black pennies and spoke, Get your b-hole ripe, son. Tonight I am Andromeda.

I giggled so hard through my front nose that the men's restroom filled with snot. The service at the café on our next day's return was much more prudent. Free vanilla paste.

The father slapped his palm on the mother's wig. Her abortions rewound back up her skirt. Dander fat of the places she had squatted changing her own diapers for a year in glass. High fives until her cervix dilated. Banished servile through the pond, a priest wrote its way free. Ultrasound dislodged the light bulbs. She released sukiyaki asswood. She milked the goats in steroid activated sphincter growth. The neighborhood became one twitching mind around her biology. She wanked tremulous on satellite backs. Techno. The news anchor's mouth exploded the syphilis that blinded ten of my eyes during the underfunded partial-birth abortion that brought this life regrettably closer. My head jutted from the fissure in veiny spasms, craving speculum and dish, suction and looky-here. She nursed spittle and cocaine across dry babyclit.

We grew different kinds of strong.

The father poured kerosene on the shell of our pet turtle. *That momclot'll turn funny if a flame survives.* The squat legs oared with lessening panic through the match strike to escape, toenails soupy clack. Carrying the fire's weight, the turtle paced itself with *a supertemporal comprehension of temperature.* The shell melted into a sideways L. The father peeled off bubbling slop-bits, bare egg. The inner-body, revealed, smacked of teal grease, and paddled, still ablaze, partway along. The oblong shiver flagging towards our boot, mouth ajar from the exposed nerves shredding stance in permanent animal quiet, which the father admired with so much hopping his foreskin dripped an extinguishing amount of yeast.

With my learnt nostril I lifted the turtle off the kitchen tile in tines of blonde. The turtle-back bore a vaseline inscription of the names and dates of men it had crawled inside in search of the first page of this book, which was different before Dad came in and shat it up with English.

I carried the turtle into the orange observatory off the second attic. The chocolate window spumed to rust and buried with it the ten wicker playmates I had scoured from the neighbors' houses among the week of BBBBurn. *I'd bound their hands with black molasses, filled their cheeks with margarita salt, crossed the false mother from their mudpacked sternums.* We sucked mom off. I could smell the adobe deathmounds from kindergarten with the teacher's arm way up my rantz. I closed the curtains made from granny's "One Time I…"s across the room. The color of raw blessing.

I carried the turtle into the trash compactor the father had used to dislocate his past, to incinerate the minivans my first quarter swaddling had spit up in, used as a sleep chamber on the cleft nights when my mother's barking horny overflowed the master bedroom.

I did a fucking killer Frank Lloyd Wright impersonation. I did Saturn. I fell on hard times.

The father's sternum became crushed exactly twice: the first emitting by birth moan in B-minor, the second my last female ejaculation in P-solo. The father had taught himself his backbone's recreation reading flipbook versions of the bible he and I had fished from Cracker Jack: one verse per metric ton. *(1) For weeks after the first crushing, the father toured the cul-de-sac for toddlers, exhibiting his new mashed potato testes jewelry. Deafening beg. (2) For months, the father sang in neuter choir until he purchased replacement organs from fashion magazines. (3) Further complications of the father's recreation had taken place over 18 nights of anal beading, during which my vision learned to stain the inner lips of fortune cookies in strip mall Chinese diners owned by those who at night slit their wrists and died again.*

I placed the turtle into the screech basin and kissed him where I thought his forehead could be. His labret piercings slewed a pudding banquet, which I consumed, then closed the lid. I pressed the smother button with my liquidated sneeze formed as a hand. The basin overflowed and burned the floor. It ate my flesh. Encased the sink. Stirred methadone into the grits I'd be having for last supper. Threshed rice inside the neo-nursery. I overheard the wicker beings in the attic ask my doppelganger into sodomy. I overheard the father's keyboard fingers ripping open. The father bragging up his birthright's echolocation. He beat the mother's lovehandles into an oblong remote control, which he used to order pay-per-view on the screen laid in the cranial wall inside the mother's 17,000th john—*You Win!*

The pay-per-view was my 17,000th abortion, under blacklight—*You Win!*—the one where before the child comes out the room is filled with chicken. Of all of my wrecks, this was the one for which I'd been invited into now, all draped in lunchmeat symphony.

My strangulated brainstem curtaining mammalian slideshow. Nights the mudflap ruptured tuna, my pillow timed itself as rigor mortis. The father ballparked my colon for the device.

When the moustache-broke-in-gravy came out reeking origin I longed for whatever wasn't in the room with me on the rare occasions waking up became insulin. I poked the dreamy pimples clogging the father's big vas.

The father snapped his fingers. I slurred my skin at the chewball. Decades followed. 19 passed the wipe. We knelt in a daisy chain toward Mecca. Looking up the mother's anus, she up the father's, malting, kaleidoscope of forthcoming sisters sliding soot Ground Round. Barber's pole hemorrhoid patched with carpet dragging behind her wheelchair. We took turns swabbing the floor with Preparation H. I leaked toward my nose a suckle family, decade plopping heirloom athwart the glisten. *Hallelujah*, the father burped, *I'm genteel*. The mother blew a bubble with her alimentary canal. It hovered over the dinner table forever.

Her leakage defined our council, registering positions in chronological vicinity. *Dayum*!

While I tested peanuts, adolescent girls vomited for any sign of my erection. They, in turn, shoved three cigarettes where I imagined the last auntie's cunt would facilitate nutrients through the gravefields of dirt we always only saw.

The father stood behind me with the bullhorn. His pelvis cut into my knees. '*La quados maneos' is Portugese for 'How about you ten-ton faggots eat my black ass out with a rake!' I picked that one up from David Koresh. My girth leads to his mind.*

Through the far door the second room was spinning. I groused my dimples against the father's mount. The speaker cone braised my neck meat in the shape of tiny mirrors, each reflecting full disco halls of hammy brunch. I crunched the glass beneath my boobs. Peanut butter in my stink yard. Sandwiches for days.

The mother moved behind the father and made his reach-around eject a broom. She took to curing our bed linens, sweet spit folded into grooves. Inside my pillow she located the mile-long lanyard I'd made at sickcamp using the director's midwife's ashes—*no escape*. The mother stuffed the broomhandle into her left ear. Out of her mouth disrobed the Ajax. She began to scrub the floor. Her knees were bloodlight. My quim erupted. My quim's quim erupted seven times. My pussy died.

The father fingerpainted an ocean on the ceiling, foam bright orange, floating fat with further speakers from out of which our Announcement whined: *Glitch rectum to be re-uploaded in seven minutes. The Twister mat is pissy. All childs farted from any womens are to have been named and renamed JEHOVIH. Place mind in mind. Place tits on itching. The injector should be installed at an acute angle to the vibrator at both ends. I can't eat clean gash no matter how I focus. Every kneecap by this evening must be re-shat. Bye. Bye. Bye. Bye. Bye.*

The father erased the ocean with his tongue ring. The father drew it all again. The ocean this time poured from the ceiling to the roomfloor where no wives were waking up. The liquid had hints of a more private Taco Bell.

The second Announcement came through my upper lip: *Bleet erupters for New Easter, please remember. Cock wallpaper in the nursery by next New Birthday Year. State mandate has me sopping. Happy forty-four thousandth of New July: wake with the rupture in your temple, mashed with chaw of Grandma in her lactose-induced coma chrome. Oh, here's your upload.* [The blather tooted through the house, the slap of half-halves on the air made bumpy with the tromboned injection sent from liquid helicopters overhead. I shit one inch from out of each wheezing direction. My pussy rose again. The father fainted.] *Sure, sure, get your strength on. Strap on your Sad Suit for Happy Nowhere. Be sure to mark the proper eye for gouging (right or left) underneath your second scalp: if you do not choose, we will choose both. We will regardless. Happy New Sputum Rupture Scene, Happy New Hypermind Deformity Cauldron, your gravy is underneath the clouds. Happy Organism*

Lengthening by .01% for which we will deduct the price out of your child. Happy Exit Sentence Grammar. Happy New Clean Cleaning. New Finally. New Him.

Swung from my knotted labia, the father spilled cookies. He blew the wall a kiss in vacuumed frequency. The father swallowed glass off the wings of moths in the lamp-gouge giving light. His protons inched Vagisil through the royal boy chum of Gilles De Rais, who he recounted in the salad spoon reflection niglet-mannered and petting the bellows of the device that incubated a century reinventing the degradation of pussyskin. The factory later sold his taint to fiefdom. *De Rais was the hero of my tapestry*, he said in an Aztec voice, placing a silenced crossbow on my sternum and masturbating us both with a piece of tire. The mother contracted her pee-pouch sphincter till the room had a kidney finish. I scooped wall chowder through the hole in my larynx and vomited to taste it.

Wait. Your wife crawls penetrated in newborn crull. I portion her movements with this hand. If she refuses to sleep parallel with you, don't let her bask. Never anticipate the trademark Everection near females who chug. Secondly, these moles, formerly my eye, only seem tender. Smear me with your fourteen-inch homework, spicboy, or the factory wins. Leach under leach, we steez our slather so trickery most galore outdoes your fucking life. Such trill um-um.

As you were.

THAT I DEMAND YOU PUT THE TEXT DOWN. THAT I HAVE NEVER LIED. **THIS IS THE FATHER**. THAT I AM SCOURGE-MADE, MALE ORGASM, STANDING UP NOW AND NOW FOREVER IN YOUR FUTURE ROOMS WHERE YOU WILL GIVE BIRTH TO THE FATHER. THAT I AM EVERY LIGHT-SIZE AND THE MORNING OF IT. THAT I AM EVERREADY HORNY, MY FATTEST FINGER TICKLED THROUGH THE WALLS OF ANY OTHER KIND OF GOD BECOMED. THAT I HAVE MY BLOOD INSIDE THE BED WHERE YOU WILL RASH A FLABBING THRONE AGAINST THE WORD. WHERE HER LIFE-SAC SITS AWAITING SIZE KISSED ON THE MOUTH SORE-GLEW AND SHITTING ALL KNOWN NUMBERS SO COME-STRANGLED. THAT I AM NONE MORE MAGICKED THAN YOU'D ASKED. **THIS IS THE FATHER**. THAT YOU CANNOT UNTHINK MY NAME.

I scalped code in the father's collision. A musket-happy pox surfed his yawn headfirst, vesicular crunch-rain. We showed the toddler's webcam nonstop sprocket. The mother born from her disappearance in the placement of a second diaphragm. None of us fucked her since the kiddie pool exploded. We found no dipteral plug.

The daughter returned from Introspective Boyfriend Practice and showed our paintings her gums with the ass of a hammer. She stood in the vestibule, reciting entitlement by country, tacking up her anus-wrinkles to empathize with the old, placing her period on moldy charts.

Across the fade she squeezed her every bacteria. Crabgrass I collected. In fiber tunic beards within the marrow her jaw sprinkled dookie-shards replacing the puzzle they once let her nibble.

She tattooed THUGLIFE on her cancer. I did my *Sinatra*

hates his toothbrush. Tread-marked, she loosened tendons from her calf, uselessly dabbing, and showed me how they operate: constantly sliding forward against her will. I bit the strings to serenade. Loving her, I grew fond of pig racket. She tucked a circumcision behind my ear.

She aired out her skin graft in full view of my room.

We had the organism on the table. Lymph and bone of graves dug up in mother moaning, tickle-drunk. We Hustler-fisted up some wonder from her all holy. She shouting, "Fuckin' howngry! Howngry ma!"

Soon we had the look we'd always wanted in our blood.

The father sent his wife to bed for class.

The wine came back up and made a windmill. I prayed Yes.

The father touched his head against my shoulder, aping tender—and on the air we shared our regal lice, a ticking dome encombed with time-bait. The father sunk his head into my head flesh. Inside my skin he bit: teeth perforating cells I'd treasured, opening my hormone doors. The father only ever wanted the greatest thing for all the me inside me. This I knew.

This.

"Please… my whole hole… needs… yours."

There was still nothing where we'd planned to say there was a lot.

I prayed.

In the bed shed the mother had become Christmas. The night that night was every horse. I prayed. Her ex-ankles shuddered with the cloning. I heard her glitter in my mouth. Her voice wriggled door jambs on my gone organs. My womb held the remote for all our sex and second lives.

I made an entry mark with safety scissors on the husk between my double's bumps. I prayed reversed.

In fright, my moustache moved inside me to wait tables. All we served was Anne. The father ordered each thing on the menu one after another, sending each one back for growing old. On the bill, writ for gratuity, he scribbled in clear ink: *Your forearms are so nice. Let's offer thug rap classes. Come home with the weed.* I tucked the paper wet into my panties. *Damn, girl, yo pussy be American as fuck!* Still I would not share such size while on the clock without a waiver.

And my pajamas at the Sistine window, bawling: "I cannot make the light not *not* divide."

I heard the father's colonoscopy backfiring. His anal-most biovalve collapsed taffy. The doctors were arguing about the size of his oil. I frequented my shame. They tugged, roping, shook off, drippy.

A doctor fired swabs at my nut. *Cum on this tinfoil until it barks out a fish.* He bent from the door, lining a needle against my dickhole. I steadied his hands. The gauge synched my urethra with swallowing feel, tapping a little pee out. He broke in, swishing force by suction, heavy the more penetrated weight the glans withheld. Almost wide enough to sing. Almost deep enough to please. *Hey, fatherplace concoction of gravitational collapse and star-star*, he spat down echoing the mucus from every carton of milk that had ever settled his thirst. The mother poked in her own subculture. Several squirts happened after my faint. I awakened floating with the balloon inside. The smiley-face inside. They made money from the blue print. They got on the floor and called it an egg.

I hacked the doctor's robe until he went downstairs, assembled some tea, left it to boil, and walked permanently from the house. He skipped through pork, fastened to several of my tracheotomies. I wore his slippers on my hands. He exited via helicopter.

Oft skullworn weathers my people caress. Bubbling their whole span Xerox. No, I say. Schlep that orb like race forgoes you and your bestest zillions shall become. I'm a doctor. Doctors fuck with gravity.

Burred there in the white there, in the pituitary dwarf. I kissed placenta in the barf of me I'd barked up from sun damage and vein-tease, shouting Father. *In the drum room of the surface, the scalding after tremble realm.* Milk waves did beer runs through and through me.

My organ donor did not want to tee-tee. We needed banjos. The father had me by the muzzle, glued in the spic-only Arby's underneath our yard. I'd had so many ways to say the one thing that would hold me up against the light and I'd deformed them all. *The very great lather of axes in a man's hands.* I had come down again regardless from all of this.

The father had me in his everymind. He could not recognize his plasticine thumbprint, the Pasolini'd bubble of his wiving. I tried to speak again into the language of his chub. I still had the fountains I'd inhaled forever. The father's backbone strangled in my craw and all of us so wiped we were inside, while throughout the house the beds were woke and rose their grievances upon us.

I knew I'd need to clean my hair—to mask my snatch in terror, decades of ex-infants at the window coughing on ballgags, the platelet mustard. Twee sugar ovens of our need for doing screw. I tried to say the father's name again. I tried to say the father's name again to scare the airport in the dishwasher. The guillotines all aimed and missed me.

The choir had been privately arranged: ten white men in white doorways, pinched in the wrath of faceless safes.

Please let me please out of this piano.

Against the house's roof above us, our leaving skin was coming down.

By piston exfoliate, my hand grew and romped the father. I dribbled his trimester. My exploding-head syndrome flourished oleaginously. I knew to rip the catheter free. Each thrust removed a square of flesh, interior of sac, and finally brought pounding through the widened piss groove, like a wrong-way babyhead, the smiling countenance of the father standing bedside. They shared a wink.

The afterbirth passed, changing sizes. I stood languid about the porocele dent. The hole never shrank. I could fit four fingers inside it and, upon completion of the fifth, shook hands with another pre-developed son or father. Smegma rocketed a tower backwards up the gall...*to be climbed later, sons. Mid-op son. I'll teach you how*...the father lifted the mother by her abdominal obesity and accused her of liking Vietnam.

They brought us our swaddled new addition, hung by its blanket. We swore to love it, but left it there. I stopped using my nose and had a cushy stroke against the car.

I could not replicate the rooms.

The house map crowning in my hidden glistening lymphoma. My hand would not fit far enough up in my skirt to balk the wraith meat. I rubbed off ages 3 to 33.

In fluid friction taught from stalking everything, I pinched my mind inside the closet. My bones were boning. The barking map welled up in my mound ramp like Era Camp.

I could not replicate the rooms, but OK.

Another coat hanger made a fancy rattle for the stepchild my liver had absorbed.

I could not find the button for the father, for his sainthood, his mental rhinoplasty cash. Each of our hairs would stretch for miles connected to the thudding twin of us we'd buried underneath the bedroom where men would come to execute their girlfriends. Out of the blood grew new employees. I'd caught one wrapped up in my clit tar. He kept alive for several brutal Sundays until our aging smudged him out.

A panel somewhere in this house. My machine to wreck a center. My oceanliner hive-sight. I came thirteen hundred times in want of dread. I am a donor.

In the living room's third layer, I unraveled the ice-colored curtains where the women always hid first, how my mother had survived. There were so many other names for mother—I was not allowed to say a one but which she said to use to dial her when she's dead. I knew which secret name when spoke would overturn the index of all evenings like Max the Sexless had in my favorite plague film. I would not let the language brown my teeth.

We made a loveassed inundation, each of us speaking, "I have laid down in the skin lamps of Nicaragua chewing crud grass in want of erupt. I have blessed the walls of any church where light came through the slaves, where the finger bread stayed smudged because it couldn't."

Of course the father interrupted: "Dicksuck jambalaya!"

Silence, Father.

The house map blistered in my mind. "We will unwind the other houses in the name of our deletion's amazing perseverance."

Now there were five maps. Now there were forty. Now.

Geofuck, groped of boilers, slushing crank, had regions. We tapped our uber chlamydia on valves. I nipped behind the mother's frown, spanking buckshot, fully charmed, and rolled a whistle in. The mother was in the test room, leaking a mountain of glam.

The sirens everywhere that never stopped stopped, so I crawled under the boiler in miniature protest of the shape of our forthcoming mausoleum. The hoot my spine concocted. I took willingly upon my comportment the manmade weather of every building.

The father brought a clipboard, bird-called. He insinuated the pretty contaminating fire was pretty. He spoke in the polyps that fed him. He sighed, asking why our leftover screw no longer made the air yogurt. He said *the art is stuffing loss*. Then he wrote me up for coagulating.

The atriums I delete store nowhere. That's how you find. How come I cling no allotment, even wife. If you my wife, dislocate something.

Obviate as condition, cunt.

I thought shooting him was acceptable because he already had gun scars. I thought crawling in those scars to live was what all teachers meant.

The infant kissed the ground. Its heart pooled up between its shoulders, cussing maiden love of mine I'd made to mimes and sent to goose the streets for softcore. The father sledded through the room in wobble arrows, mocking the Invocation Queen— who in her vast batter blown unfolding had the night dead in our mind. "I am tired of this voice and yet I speak."

In retribution I drank a box of lipid water and threw it up into the shelves of book: the ink still wet inside them, drooling no matter what long years. Our horoscope in leather cities. Our Barnes and Noble shunt.

More maps wobbled further up my blood.

Love me.

Love me.

Love me.

The father and I chewed through the volumes one by one. He sweated captivating tea. His voice straddled above us, re-shingling the sour roof, "I just caught us a torture nigger! I am a torture nigger!" His hands were by my sides. He looked through my one eye, then the other. He turned the saws on.

I did not feel like having butt-dinner before High Prayer. This is why I'm not the President.

We ripped the pages of our ages' number each out from every index. I fed my pages to one infant or another, so much I could not spore down and enough gasoline to nap. From his, the father folded replications of the mother and scribbled dick jokes on her spine.

"Eat the map, babe."

In their silence, the infant and mother's bodies shat back our pages in perfect, equal inches the further we fed each in.

The father had his own ideas, though he would sell them soon for free to raise our funds for Conflagration.

THE WORMS DICTATE MOTHER IN MY CROWN. I AM THE SPERM LUSH. ON THE GROWTH BY SWILL AND EARLE, BURSAS CLUMP.

YOUR PARASITES ARE DREAMING OF A BIGGER HOST.

I THROAT THE HOME. PORTIONING LOVE. HATCH THE FINISH. DNA GREASE WHITES MY PEDDLE. HONKY OINKING TEXT. MOUNT AFTER BABES HIVE GOING BURR NO MORE PET SPREAD VISION.

GRIND THE COMA DOWN TO DRINK.

I AM THE SEXTING ZILCH OF BATHS YOU LOST. WALK MY BLOOD ON A LEASH. FOR YEARS I ATE DINNER ON A BILLBOARD OVER THE FREEWAY, ASPHYXIATED BY THE PERFUME OF CARS. I WASN'T CURRY GAMED IN PARADISE SWOLLEN ROWS.

THE IMBRAEL FRISBEE FROM YOUR DANDRUFF.

In the oxblood yard the wire gates should shudder open.

The sermon graft had been recoiled, my thorax funneled into delusion locations, sold at fractions of their worth. The audience of dead sperm children crowded turkey too. Teeth white as corpse glue. We had forgot how to unwin.

In the yard my rectum drew sundamage.

With the leopard, chugging anal milk. Scab rooms soldered over where I'd taken pictures of my mother's puncture against raw slate. The father above us in the sandwich costume with paper crusting on his state-owned arms. I could smell the calcifying muscle, the grind of Granddad light, men in wicker hordes. The father had been sworn in as their leader. I wore their names among my birth tattoos. Crammed in my walls where nothing listened. Crammed in confetti under the son of Xanax.

In the yard the grass had grown erupting, sculpting lesions from my bedtime.

My platelets draining skyward, up into the ox, the ox then raining into me. I heard the father call the men's names one after another, though through my flood flaps each name precisely mirrored. The men, when called, came to squat upon me, earning $$$ for the encouragement of cancer. My gut flowed quickly with their liquidated heaping. *This one's for Texas. Mine'll flypaper her lungs.* The father watched in denim, slitting his neck in envy over all.

In the yard above me, packed in active OCD meat, the father crushed the skull of every sperm between his rubbered thumbs.

My hair went curled. The men were gnawing all together pinker tracts between their tracts. The auctioneer sang his confession through his youngest Indian identity, risen of the land to become the land. The light erupted sand showers on the lawn, coagulated instantaneously as furtive language and popped our skulls off. In the light there was the torpor lotion. On the topmost floor, I killed my hands.

I peeled my tattoos off, re-swam the birth canal. Harpoons flummoxed directions the pound wore. Worry an inward pulse the mother flecked. The tapeworms inside my come rubbed their purple up her buck. The father squatted the previous day, corners revolving skin tags, slushed beige ninja stars. *Now we're getting somewhere*, the father lied.

Neckblood of swans deluged my fuck-welt. I stoked hospital in the father's yum. He opened, supple gal, his vinyl nest. Nostalgia busted through his jury, let him keep the grapple of his toot in my previous ambitions. I performed séances in his wank. He screamed from handstands we were too fat to deliver, pointing first at the mother, last the moon, *some poor excuse for longevity*.

Cram the soil pennies before growing, chased from heartburn with a stamp, gloating in our acids, winded and yelping feed. How I beat you means the moon. How he lights the marks I give. I drown myself in what we do. You are no son unless I'm blind and by the falter of your voice this family is lead black and further. Cultures farm us.

Cow-pie is your troop. Your mandrake mother sung excreted from the waft, faggot, racist, leave our house.

I rim-jobbed a blast of aunt from sanctioned dandies.

Our pyramid awoke to rising while I was through with growing old. Our unwinding minds re-rendered fettucini alfredo wallpaper.

Our pyramid had 17,000 sides, which made it not a pyramid.

Its index glistened in the bilespeak ejected by the sun's emerging skull.

Each eye had an eye, a butter outlet.

Pigflesh cornucopias sang raw shit and hid our words.

The father and the mother threw themselves in condensation where on the pyramid they could reach anything. Their flesh grew bubbles on their backs, popped in the pinning of where the want burst in their lungs: *glog-caloris-lumdis-lumdis colors*.

The auctioneer emerged among the mumming gathered masses

who'd come to press their teeth into our soil, each ill-wept one of them ecstatic with the automatic weapons woven in their ribs. He raised his claws. I could feel my eggies prancing. Weeping ready for the leap.

Our pyramid tattooed and slathered and ejecting licorice-scented wreathes of fire. In the weekend eons after these would hang hung in the houses of the kind.

In bursting of the father's skinbeats in the rosebush his language photographed the air. A nicotine dome formed around the airspace where other years had let the yard turn white. The sperm burst on my lips and then were more mirrors, again re-halving halves.

I watched the pyramid condense against the northeastern awning where sticky rice blooms sparked on our amnesiac piddle.

What I could have fed. What I could have had to feed on.

I moved to stand against the slurring pyramid kissed by our earth in slut of worship.

Doorbell, I said inside myself with both hands shaking. I heard a dictionary spread.

Dad meat, I said aloud towards the father, though there wasn't any left.

I replaced the dust with landmines burnt lard from the scour she had planted sly rapes gaunt about the live-long question and opened perspective graves (her hide-and-seek-bait and fuck-me-cuckoo-tome) with shovel ditty. The girl most street in pearling worship weighted under us. I should have seen her skeleton coming. It dried before I met her.

Gentlemen.

By accident the device began dissipating menses. One of my leakier hips stopped working. The Jell-O of several neighbors lessened when I spat. I slid a maxi pad over each eye and kept digging. The cheese glans surging from my armpit shunted burlap.

I shook the bones privately in a damaged garden. I constructed a monument no family could soil, no memory could pussywhip. I forgot where and of what, and lazily gnawed the femur.

You fitted the skull in one of your pussies and it grew bigger with appreciation. I fitted the skull coming out of you back into my mouth, for it was soft now, and became glad. I broke her ribs across our mirroring eyes and could remember. I sank with you, alone now, cheerleading into the sand, holding my hands out empty, around you. Sinking as we swelled, our gestures, larger than the backyard, said lonely things about her. Saddled between our hips, the skull began to smile. The teeth replaced the ground and the cavity we were standing in made us one in the battle against tartar. The everlong stew we forced upon those who didn't need us. We fused cradle cap and sinew to the brick outside our hunger. I offered you her shrapnel in a light that barely held us. We spilled forth the braying molecular politic of having.

In split-level of the hour, the pyramid destroyed the seam, turning the sentences of our mourning into alsdkf oashid uohasoiudhy98 auyer98ryhauheur ha;oiudh; fahsd;jfha suhdfpua p;ufha;sjdh ;fjhas ;djfh; ouashdfo;ahs;dofha;osdh ;ouahs;douhfa;osuhy uayuh ;aushd;jh ;ash;rhea;orh;aehr.

The house stretched through its center. Terrific! The wall paint ruptured sleeves that I will wear to see you through. I could no longer fit my head inside the knee room where our K-mart portraits slashed to moon rocks. Where in years chewed white by the father, we would sit and kiss each other's meat until it was all over the online. *To make the house the house's home ungone again.*

The new foyer's floorboards wept each time I bent over, my grease scouted by the leavened scrim of levitating exits. Doors with clitoral hoods and handles rolled in wax paper mimicking whoever came to them's #1 juicebox celeb. The door kissed by my last child's hands was shook to black gas. Its throttle warmed my body dumb. Snot in chocolate leakage for the pleasure of democratic belief.

Us silent in the scabbing hallway pouring shit like five of Christ.

This, my bedroom, with the stirrups, and the paneled bleachers stuffed overboard by chunky puppets. The men left encamped inside the father where he burst through all his horse suits like a dickface overall.

I crossed the room dressed in white pork cut from the ribs and bust of every human thought I'd lived through ever in a loop.

- In the attic the diagrams did melt. The scabs of new tickle time making ice form around our bisexuality. The bathtub posh with ruby family skinsuits. *This length covered my lids and lined my throat.* Dressed in the drapes, I unwalked backwards, bent to bursting gasoline dew all through the years.

- In the threadbare stairwell I made lipids out of begging and mailed each in gray awaking to whatever name slipped from the pen.

- On the scum bed I again allowed the apse up my idea of me as a child who'd never had a need. *The rattle of it lasted long enough so they could generate a mile-thick rewind for all the rest of you.*

- In the kitchen the mother had took to marriage

with her gloved hands in the bee-loved earth now.

- This blood hid inside the endless paper compromised with edges.

That was it. The whole born-again regatta.

In the lid room I crushed my skull against the sky.

The father cured the mother in brine for letting him feel proper. Cross-fluted by high caliber autographs, the silent topography of his recoil went BONEFUCK.

I'll tell you potbelly sonnets if you comb the Judas from your hair, the father scolded his ingrowth.

In the symmetrical permanence of discharge, the father vetoed cotton for any excuse. *The spleen is here to stay,* he insisted, pulling the trigger against another sentence of shortly hopped morph to Dodo mating.

We handled his execution with floppy hugs. I tuned into him for the keys. In the yam handle barn, invoiced opulence became my motto. Anemic mottos were bong. The full Tonka cabaret proselytizing us.

The cry we could not taste.

Far creepier lawns, divorced by pendulum. Our house poised its la la. Our fertilizer told futures. One day I got under the mother and impersonated a hole. She followed into me for miles until the marriage took place on the cowl of our exploded birth.

The father ripped himself in light in glistened shards, the pig limbs of his jailbait body double so much stronger than he'd ever been, arranged in wax, curling through the center of the father's chest in colored cavities he'd had sawed out of my mouth. Through my dumb brown wet split-mouth the father spoke Kaslever, language he'd scribbled in my school books with the pigment of my monthly blood, the incantations worn on my forehead at school eating sack lunch, the same bruise-lipped paisley tongue-text that from the ex-homeland diorama in the attic had by now begun gushing in gold loam—curing the pyramid to splinters where it kissed the cleanest, hieroglyphic spittle gifted in waves against my lungs—my lungs aching with the spit-up of the voice shorn straight through me, mega-white—begging—pursing—peeled in gag reel slideshows in and on and through the walls: *God damning the cervix fountain father in the sight of no sarcophagus. God damning the jaguar puppet and powdered milk in sky'd curtains. God damning my disrupted scrotum. Gog damning the wet weight west dream dentist in the Broca's area of this sentence. God damning God damning the left* *handed pilot of the drum circle center. Jehovih damning the deleted scene of Invocation of My Demon Brother, in which I and my many many would have had appeared in blue, raw around the knees for centuries in the dicksuck witch tent with the sandwich fixings duct-taped in halos of my brain. Jehovih damning the 17,000th room basted in spittoons of this long blood pyramid's 17,000th corridor, sunk through the bedroom of my remoaning, where in 17,000 weeks I will have asked 17,000 times, for the index again to be God damned again and again again to be God gone.*

In my inhalation then, thereafter, the doors throughout the pyramid bruised closed. The father's thorax hid the light as it remained, from the ovens, from the nut. The father pasting the scrim lengths of his inseam with the stem drip from what had come out of the mother bashed again against the baking wall, one repetition for each syllable pushed out of my body into the blonde spume. The father in knee boots and white sled gloves. The father in 17,000 bibs of the same color. The father in me demanding of the father:

STAND UP, SHIT, AND TURN AROUND.

DRESS MY BLOODMIND IN EXIT BATTER.

BECOME SMALLER.

HAVE ANOTHER CHILD.

The father sampled war, remixed bye-bye. He struck poses saluting pi with typhoid smarminess. Tasting: *an indigested maze of suggestible guinea rollicked here, 9 o'clock, G's.*

I wandered about my outrigger dawn, hefting dog tags. We scratched a tank up the child hill. The father, pepped about Hitlers, grabbed a blanket. We skipped ethnicities across the sun.

The civilian I fornicated with a wizard barrette dribbled financial loans into a sock. Some trough of parents with dysentery squared the driveway. I trickled digested weathers, unknown temperatures, proto-tyrannies. I honed my flap to expel enamel. My fistfucker came back wearing a gold bracelet.

Tuck the sleet so goon. We college up our jock-straps. We cement-wrestle our boo. Our circulations ease.

We prayed real slow for napalm. What our lungs had wasted

finally became injected fuel waved through houses we couldn't bring ourselves to pet goodbye. The clouds were gritty cake. Our ears squirted Ranch dressing. The light by which we caught survivors.

The mother went outside and pretended she was having a million backward labors. These became the planes that would always haunt us.

On his knees, the father, in the who-got-killed hair net. We made more we. The googoo phrase hosed our silver hairs down. The father with a spigot from his abilities, bloating the center of our house and all the houses grafted around it, nativities where on the air and earth for miles in rungs and pillows the clog of other fathers spurred cake in pews of fright. The father spoke in rungs.

"Forgive that I might stay the father here forever. Forgive that I have dressed the light bulbs in verse—that when the pony opens on the table, slow unfolding, there is no inch of me I won't gift.

"I can not recall you here, my other body, my quick-tattooed eruption, child I have seen sent looped at my tongue into the four folds of any camera, where they come to touch the lid for happy urge-day and touch again.

"As when as when the first asp slithered from my jawbone I

recognized its hum. Likewise, when your cleft cousins's second sac's physician asked me for ten minutes off the record, I begged my ocean in his ear.

"I have never seen a pig I could not cripple, yet I have chosen how, instead, to mate: with both eyes burnt and throat in egg fleece, my backbone blistering our wonder."

Having spoke, the father held enormous font, though what came out came out white and wingding. The father's skin fit an accordion no one knew quite how to play. Our laptop hid in the kitchen full of cookies and camouflaged itself with knives, untyped forever. I put my left arm on the father. I sledded my armpit skin to fit into his and thrust it, our dummy limbs lashed and laughing walls we let the house hold until we had time all to ourselves.

The father's hand in my hand, I gave us matching dancing parent blisters. I undid his studded faux-punk belt. Whipped me blackened by the shoulders. I wanted to. I whipped me till my hair fell out in prison rhythm. I was. The mother underneath me catching squirties: her lips, too, plastic, grubbed in weak milk pity, pushing out of her, too, gone, kid sick—*though beneath her there was no one there to spill.*

We hung in the house with letters moaning and newer floorboards warped with where they were. We turned to look through ourselves and though the paper, masturbating in the name of names, please, "Let us grow."

The father popped and locked, full investigation. Readers incubated the gown of his smaller effort. He reeked of the recently mourned. His index of ejaculations set in skid mark. The father explained adolescent chum. His wigs receded. He cupped his puke to raise it.

Doing the Egyptian bride with a CD case, the mother spanked of epicenter. I lost her in the haze issued from mouths the daughter we uncovered kissed. The mother was speaking midnight, unable to turn around, and I held her from a distance in a stance that said I had to – her length not dissimilar to the daughter I grew up as in another mind. The shrank imitation not an incest quiver, yet still the same the slather did, we remained condensing through dark apertures, hovering just above penetration, until she said we needed milk.

I noticed a lot of heads craned in varying attitudes of ironic permanence and so armed myself accordingly with the intention of carpet-bagging suicide to the ground zero I was conceived upon and clit-sang the alphabet in a dying strobe.

I heralded atmosphere that really wasn't.

I shucked the skin off sainthood. The pyramid encrypted its retort all overhead. The disease soldered to the lawn of white where under which the second turf stutter-shifted its prisms of mammals de-imagined to give us room to pant. Grogweight of the mothers in the sun house soiling the Smart Carpet as they ate windows, all inner lids writ with text mistranslated here from page 1 through whatever page this is. All decade infants cuffed and cauterized, carousing high five with a fist formed out of shitheads. Soft whip of lung butter where all through the sour milk of this Dream Drum Day the device had malfunctioned in the den, the scruff of our peoples' ten million puff-paint sweaters forced on fast and all at once over our heads: neon garments bearing our neon names and our expressions scribed in scissor flab and foamed with whatever felt casual.

A strong, slow cold.

On my own chest, the nipples caving with Dad lecture: "What is the gun of years. What is the Stoning Fortress Person. The liquids we had camped on in blackbears' crotches for geek forevers. The locked lock will not unbe itself. The same door to the door's door embossed and buried in our natural egos."

Ours. In ours. Dubbed us up double. The pyramid birthing a new food: sexskin socks and witch snot cotton candy. Feedback vaginas whipped in light and incense crowns to wear to drown soon. Gold-plated aura panties. Exit Special rice lungs. Tumtum bunnies baked in glee saliva if you've got the funds. Halfies nowhere hunting along. *What* fucking *is this?* Dad kept squealing. I knew. I had it memorized where my bug was: **New Eat Here Ever Only Buffet install locations bashed up through driveway pavement for all homeowners. Eternal Service: valet skin sacs, scald skin sac dress code, stem upload menus pierced nasal b/w anvil lottery, Nanny Rites, pre-dining swordscape carwash birdbaths arousing feline waiters over cream of Geofuck Charles, listening troughs barfed full by bruised white women in white baptism chatbot shawls!**

Laugh, bitch. Laugh. I was enchanted.

I climbed a ladder of infected kidneys. Toward the girl I used to be. Vaunting her constipation by knots measured my reflection. I held the crime of her disowning, her expiration date peeled off a kernel in the waste, dictating the day she left, listing the time of her funeral services, jealous of what I later did to the exhumed toy.

I fondled her diabetes. It became the room where I gave my word. I stabbed rust into her G spot. It spun time long enough to see her decompose. The face went off the money she had set between us.

I got over it. I sucked the belly of a starving fawn. I tore the genitals off a nursery. I slit my rabies with Clyde. I flocked through Africa sizzling sores. I circle stomped a vulva. I lynched, looking good in photographs. [Knees stuck bent above the fire, hopping toward what little sky befell him, the father's hobby sword.]

I salad-tossed the father into hibernation. He took praise and criticism in the same piss. The pollution he versed stroked an ampersand from my throat.

Above the above, my dog upload through the infant made the pyramid go blank. I could see it spinning great mediocrity. The pus preacher at its center mandating words our eyes would force to cancel. Laminating every other sickness where the pudding pop pumped in the child for dollars. Wad cauterized where we'd made no suggestions, a noise-hole sunk into its own fascism. *The second Father swallowed in my courageous film of headlocks framed in all alone mirrors. The undulating fallout.* In ash, our last skin laundry fell bib-white from an unfolding sky doormat.

In the cream rinse of the house I showed my cunt to Rommel and he cried.

I approached the house wall from the outside. I put my head against an inch. Threw up. Drank the throw up. Threw up again, My hands aped tacks. My butt was always geeking. My backbone chanted through my nostrils and wet my dress.

Overhead, the negroids in the summer, dilated, dangling from the other sky's skin lining by their toes, a sunburned blackness at the center of their shaved chests, spelling my name in chode Morse code. The largest negroid threw up Crips, his fingers knotted how the weekends had before we gave up the concept of forcing breakfast. His stoma'd twin reached to touch me in my no-no delight dump spots. My forehead pitched a tent inside it and the negroids climbed in. Their bellies beating forced Ligeti through my apse on some Entrepreneurial PCP. In the glint of rust I could see where Ligeti's yummy unveiled the raptured women from The End before our start, their napes all sewn together in the jawbones of us young. When they would blink my scalp became prismatic, a bitch's dream.

Through the house wall I heard the father drinking back each inch that he'd rejected. He would perform the wake on my final birthday, which lay in wait against the house in such kind tangles of goatbodies, mashed by yours.

The father wiped his mouth of the OAHSPE, speaking baby-juice:

The vocent leaks in separate holiday. The sassy flock mountains blood. See the anglo chud that became our session. We're nearly killed enough to see. To accidentally tell the truth by proxy of a jocular confession. However loved thy victims go. May Atari pirouette befuddle your horizons. Raise the roof, amen.

The father wore our neighborhood around his neck. It became his burnt little trophy, his ocular doodad. We folded the corners of our sight.

Bubonic innards canopied the crib. The father teased my fat with a bazooka. In a sumptuous char our pageant held. We knifed karaoke into the toaster, hawking a spell with modem chute. The atmosphere longed to do worse in our pocket, where we kept ink to replace it.

The pyramid unstuck my ticks, roiling manias blanketing the fairground. I followed sharp through heads I lost and gained, air-guitared. My profile rotted corners along the bricks baked arctic loogie.

The father creamed in canons just to tease. He beat his chest with my password. First my fingernails loosened and fanned off. The white scarred upon my breath.

Burned sun burned through the bruised back of my still replicating head as under pills the night turned thirty. The grave-praise swollen in boiling stationary. My body double's doubled body thronged with machine gun against all housewives through the holy tube. I could tell the body double from my dumb one by the Saturn tattoo cut on our scalp sunk with the *Cream Them* Mandate in it, my billioned children concrete, all of them cleft to whatever wasn't going to happen ever.

I was getting really long now. I could gift my future body on the World Wide Web once a season.

I have to go now.

Pyramids together rose from converse latitudes, scatting itchy. My mohawk with gasoline, pumping the crura off famous wives.

The missus conjured of my replacement affectation simmering waltz by waltz by bye.

I sat the new daughter auditions on my lap, fingering garlic into each and leafs the wet returned formed more daughters for the line. The auditioners ended lice in a siphon, never jag cotton yard and spurned, or so my brain declared.

Everybody's good, I wept, *now assort*, mouth humping slant geometries with a crack lighter and shuttering eyelids about the spork I used to test their squints.

One bag-eyed orphan yanked loose her front teeth and ate out my cleave from a stepping stool. I carried her until she lost her name. I spent her birthday taking a very thin wire between her

ribs. Her body lasted five days in the incinerator. With the mess
I broomed a fort to which she was not allowed entry.

The houses lit with kids in rows. The device intoning new windows into chubby Deneuve pink. To where the bunching tissue caved and we could enter us. Butter rations for the sudding shores covered in whiners who felt they'd read. Piglets insisting in tic rugburns on our chunks where we sat and chugged and rowed the fog to longer bloodplay funhouses along the light that would not rise. My cannon worships all these steakknives hidden in dinner. Throats unwound in remembrance of nannies with their fattest fingers in our enormities awaking carrot flesh in nets over old women splattered. What we had used once to build a mother in bulk. These no-orgasm sculpted lungs so in the vomit we could breathe good. A story for all gray space to wallow with and please his inner-vibrators. The house around a shaft of eggs in heavy stock. Our hallway switched so knocked out and bloodblistered I could tell at last that someone once had loved me and my Antarctica tattoo.

On the device I was derailing. The cyber-toddlers of this fair country splattered down my front butt pillows. I tried pressing the button for Hold me In Me and goddamn frottage celebration came. The mother, wet beneath, eating of me and my wrecked heirs like hot baggage drop-off. Her back was slave butter of a sweeter kind. She got full and I kept going. She rawed my divots all multi-stunk with air force collards popped beatboxed. The fatfuck mother fraught in erupt-ribbons who woke cuts between my toes and light my light out and sprayed her brain-damaging eye.

"This is not the exit," the mother said and said and said. Her digits stuck to the dollar-bill meat sent soaring out of the independent creation scene my linings had deformed because they could. Another half-hog fell from my aorta, ran to get lips.

I scratched the gush of us.

Through the window I watched the other mother polish the pyramid with neon VCRs. The food of the tapes spooled from the soft gears every dad had for doing slave squats. My nudity snarfed large planets. I took and held the only book against me hard. I left the room and came back in as anybody.

Using pliers, I scalped the mother. An asbestos perm mapped beneath the effluence. I boiled her of convexities. I devalued her morgue weight.

I shampooed the floor with autopsy. Woody Woodpecker in the shine. The scandalmonger swung. I had been passing beaks.

A sightless lap for the mother's mother where the mother came because the father held her slit balled to one point of skin in his wooden hand.

Up a tree, the mother filleted her slit with a screwdriver to celebrate having me, and fed the wad to a bird's nest vomited from where the father used to suck.

My drag fell off. I scampered blind into the device that fed my bumps chlorine. The circus that reattached Japan utilized flame throwers from a wheel chair. I took a bath until I was Japan.

All I could see was slaves.

Lard slaves cool slaves Raid slaves slaves with the white beaks buying stock ash slaves glue slaves big-as-a-store slaves slaves of mothers we buried in our hands slaves for forcefields eternal and deformed honky ass slaves slaves in college slaves like you and who you were slaves with the organism hid inside them shit slaves hay slaves grave slaves dew slaves slaves with lust beyond the years slaves in mustard slaves au jus and so sweet slaves of the shine mall slaves-to-go slaves as filler sick slaves babe slaves gay slaves slaves who cannot stand.

I held this scroll and a blue finger.

I closed my face and read the rest of all the books. My bruises gave me head.

Dream slaves slaves of no color slaves for baking cookies free slaves grace slaves bull slaves old slaves a bigger kind of slave around the eyes slaves who refuse to let you see them purse slaves slaves inside the rind of ice slaves to morning the most obese slaves you can imagine day slaves phrase slaves OS X slaves the slaves of wire and sunshine without light slaves who chugged white wine and liked it the slaves I grew.

Books drunk into my chub and left crappy questions where my cells were:

Question? _____
Question? _____
Question? _____
Question? _____
Question? _____
Question? _____

In each blank I gave your name. And I was pleasant. I was rounded in the milk.

They didn't like that. The questions, they screwed my cheeks to theirs. They fed themselves and burnt themselves and fed themselves into me through human ways I had not learned to defend.

The slaving fields got higher every sentence I remembered. *Please let me gut me.*

My skin cold rising at the sky all pickle-fried and sold so long ago.

My emblem crushed into the moon and all the slaves all grinning windows.

In that pearly enormity, there you were.

Before the mother aged all my retracted vinegar, the wormhole peeled spamjets of eon. Portioning superstition, she whispered jissom to her kin. She imposed relatives everywhere visible, prying rubies from her grease-crown.

The longest ho got her piles scissored. We canonized the booty, ornate tofu. We performed a drive-by on her manicure. Scraped her energy drink bits of whiffle.

I jowled DUI's for a sanitary lisp. The father spread his earnings on the floor. Had us humping. The cellulite we flossed with sponged, subwoofer.

The bodies coved and froze. No residual blowback. The mother and I yelped *soft* at their bangs for the father's visit-seed. The coaxial shush he gave resembled us.

My spew trained pandemic.
My growing stomas fiddle.

My prime clones gauge blow.
Crew some hide.
I, the unctuous quacker of ping.
Torque your boy.

Hoarded by our fontanels, drapery is us.

Stabbed in our scab forehead with the old wind codelocks. Bodies worshipping their mouths. MY HIVE BEHIND IS NEEDY. I HAVE BEEN SPRAYING WITH THE HORSES NOT FORGOT. My cored mind huddled under the electricity dumpster wearing grafted paisley dress slacks. In fabric razzled from the pets our lungs would ride into food. I knew seven definitive all-allowed visions in popdream dressing. Slut song dreamboy behind stabbed eyes and bitchboxes screaming Hallelujah for the device to come around again and hear me gripe. The mouths again all mouthed their mouth parts where I wasn't. MY LOVEY GIRL, I AM ENTHRONED. I WANT TO BE ALL OF COLLISION CITY GROWN RELENTLESS BEYOND DAD'S WOLFING MUSICS. THIS EXIT FORTRESS PRAYS ON EVEN HE. I didn't want to make this contribution anymore and so I did it harder. The father's blonder totem scrotum rose against the word in my all's image.

Look, a blue bird.

In my assassination bedroom blown. The gown unshit the pyramid to websites stuttering ex-breath-light over bibbled asswhip sunrise. I smudged with the first of our next 17k births and became a comedian of the High Order. At the window in the window, scolded over, someone knocked a see-hole through the scab's smile. I could count the sternums through where they'd begun to form a copy of my Christianity belongings. I could not count what I wanted to count—oh well.

Ash puttied in the birthday hut became skeet when thrown backwards.

Our gonads conjecture when dabbling one swing, when off peels the blackface and you learn me as byproduct.

The mother's legs jutted from a dumpster. She lifted the gulped snot from her three day cold, eggplant in the fatty tissue below her abdomen and ate again the toppings for the zip-lock incubation, tubercular from exiting her clouded spank, mashed full of maggots, undulating, streamers of half-progressed fetuses in the dangle.

Strafing our erection willy-nilly on her pipe-folds. The beeper signifying her pregnancies. Diamond-studded teethmarks, the lactate-tendril pillowed terror from our shiny advent.

I flavor the joust and occur rotten. Spawn which glows chosen, turgid swell, froth that vistas take, flank deed, flash

my summoning, venom. Shatter benumbed by hapless roids.
Marshal that tang. Shemhamforash a little.

I wasn't even white. Tongue-tied with some someone. My bliss-hole squirted index cards in trigger for all the dealers, our girlfriends accompanying by tongue drums:

O

PLEASE

MEGADIKK ME IN MY LARDDZ, BOI—

WHEN I'M TXT I GET THIS BIGGEST EVENING

IN ME CLOSED

ALLOVRR. I CAN UNLOCK

ANY LITTLE CITY.

OW

I AM TRYING HARD OW

TO OW

FIND THE ON-RAMP

TO THE COSMOLOGIC SHARD, AGAIN

AT THAT AND

NO OW

ONE AGAIN OW

OW
NO ONE
O
WILL OW
O
EVER AGAIN
BEAT ME
LEAVING

[My grafts in hiccups. Look up and huff it. Dry candy between us always now.]

Forgive me.

In the astrologic ballroom, the father slit his wrists with Ranch.

[Rise of urine trophy in the yard, recombining every birth-shape and lick for lick and sin for sore in the eek of wow, old babies halved with neon scoreboards demanding piercing via priest. "Every inch we've ever lathered, loving, Father." "Printless, scentless Father." "I want to bathe my ignorance."]

I could not stop the whooping blood of *WHAT WAS WASHING WHERE OUR WORMS WERE HELLBENT IN THE RIM OF ALL OLD MINDS* crowded with backs unleavened in XXXXL mirror fantasy, my skins spanned in Yes Please Let Us Sleep Here Constantly Begun.

The sky, defecating artillery, red with our stuck-together sayings, diced through varying wingspans, unkind buoyancies, toward a malfunctioning dryness, the arresting woodwork we posed our bodies into, lying to keep the symphony of unconscious oil bestrewn as days and days alone were slowing, fuck our postures nifty legend.

The mother clasped the ass-side of her panties around my face. Inkblots in the dervish, I reveled creature anatomies, removed my puncture guard. Scuba through the exposition, intestine glue hardening with unsuccessful meals, sieves clamped in bionic release through the forced fart air, my unwashed fingers prodding cat shed into the hardly responsive colon, begging the mother, the father, *please, whack the chunks through while I doze.* The food an inner-gigantism, short-circuiting scoop, waking up with it pieced somehow far into my sinuses.

My multiplying apneas.

Bubba-surge the mighty cleft. I call the ground whore if it allows beyond my step alone. Behold the smashed, gloating in their stillness. Monoliths of fester plane the Umbræ, repenteth brackish, puny in pustule. FUPAs crown the Schood of Hein. Chuck the bifid tines resplendently. Stifle what lukewarm pontiff. In the bulwark bore devoid of succor she has lost. Dagon gaggles your fane. Our pundit mackdaddy, formed and formless, emerged unending, built stagnant within.

I made my redoubled aurababy breathe me with the reams of we in compulsive creamcorn. **Exploder** lined his eyes.

In pristine gifts: our pontoon dildo pillow ejaculating cold introductory heroin.

The baby's secondhand saliva tasted female. I wanted its each inch back inside her. *I prayed & prayed & prayed* until *the baby's flayed back made more babies.*

Seeing my stunning family, the father beat the child to death. Seeing seeing, the father's mirror beat the child's death to death with the machete. Scripture worms from us unleashed. The father giggled, *Night-night.* My eggs went ridiculous. Dust-batter through the hexagonal eyeholes of our penitentiary memory.

More Than Some Quite High Number Sold!

The father pretended to leave and I went with it. *Oh yes,*

Exploder.

I opened up my Gaze of Shrine.

I disrobed the reticulated infant. I teased the good snacks out.
The table glistened.

Our Father took me by the thrall, *all seas inside me and beside
me.*

Another night with zits I could not feel.

What had I become but any mother with the Disney cavities to
match.

I shot the horse in its mouth to make it cough magic. The mother clenched dimes with her flap to cool the AIDS. A kite embedded in the hang-down.

My wounds green faster. Listing the final moan, the mother furthered her wombs and a piano key dipped out.

The six shooters I retrieved from the mother by grinding my teeth down her nape. The earwigs tinkling from our crevices utterly. The way I timed the world in stigmata.

We took turns kicking the shine off a dolphin to impose our sex.

I do handstands times the living. Ascend unto wax, ye stewards, him among the dads. Unto the father, gave with myriad bumpy, lap the fucking trapezoid. Harken some woo, giving icy. Workmen talk. Dwelling lord-huffed, appareled with furnace, I buckle midday to pharmaceuticals.

Governor of cobwebs, weave us dry.

Every female I'd believed in. Every giant gash collapsing the ill mountains. Clot where thugs would cry me into creasing how to hold you harder. I could not be and never was before and so had been. My girly boner pirouetted its rosacea on the Lite Brite we wore unending and wound it around inside into a slaughterable oven, burn turning on all in our blood and staying on and burning as long as I was never wet for fun, and only loved where dead would nail themselves to anyone who ever mattered, while all I ever knew to do is rip.

The mother, existence-crazy, shucking relativity, all her former periods converted to makeup, mask behind the landscape she toted, sons banged socket on her advancing wet.

I am the rind pussy smelting.
I am the cluck below silence.
I am hired expellant.
I am the Down syndrome beatitudes.
I make deeper. I make.
My cunt hides other cunts.
I catapult my young at earrings.
I am the accordion mammy fixit.
I wean everyone at once.
I wear a ski-mask on my sex.
I am the sake clown baking massive.
I ream the globe's flat end.
I quintuple chalk marks.
I, the dean of Botox.
My sass needs amps.

You weep to confirm physical space and I have to ruler that.
OWWOW MUSSY
OW
Brick dust allures me.
I boss your size.

The mother (me) and the mother (mine) thorax to thorax, ovums cleaved. She feels electrical. I thaw the ranks: all men our grungebutt had poured out of us no more—troops ribstuck in their eternal-earned locations of ape music, parenting replacements not quite adequately soon. Instead, some kind of game show where the moon had killed itself due to my tunnels and how I'd chose to spend my time, which had never been a choice and yet I chose it because I was born.

I let the mother do the gluegun in me for bonus credit and still heard nothing but rubbing. I grew a pucker more than any replica's true location and still I was totally all me. I now knew I had to shit, though where the worms were my swill-muscles would not flex or disappear together.

The men took to throwing the barbiturate into my flow. They rubbed each other sunward for the friction that hid our nights. Shit scooting in my tubes throughout the next ten hundred Things I Wished I'd Done A Long Long Time Ago To Everybody.

And that was that again as it would be. My many exited infants'
clear hair swaddled the pausing sound of all invention while
the remaining men charmed to waking the machines in their
surroundsound.

The machines came on and called us down. They used the voices
we'd not offered. They rose the fingers in our throne rooms. I
came forward for us as I was made to and so had always wished
and would again, but after you.

In mounds the wanting machines mashed us the fukk up!!!!!!!!!!
!!!!!!!!!!!!!!!!!!!!!!!!!!!!!!

In liquidating grunt-juice we grew more plague space like a
good boy!!!!!!!!!!!!!!!!!!!!!!!

All heat of vision baked us snarling in our masks and no one
watched!!!!!!!!!!!!!!!!!!!!!!!!

Under the sun's huge one and only blue white dickhead.

The mother admitted that being a mother meant only having loved your wife enough to impersonate her once she was gone.

Pressed until the negative magnetization of electrons our nerves mistook the hug for.

I command fashion, catwalk postpartum, corpulent floater nebulæ, barren warks accorded shape. When the scour thrones signet, chant the host dwelt on any. Your spouse belongs wholly elsewhere, said by every action.

About the Authors

BLAKE BUTLER is the author of *There Is No Year*, *Nothing: A Memoir of Insomnia*, *Ever*, and *Scorch Atlas*, which was named Novel of the Year by *3:AM Magazine* and a finalist for the Believer Book Award. He edits HTMLGIANT as well as two journals of innovative text, *Lamination Colony* and *No Colony*. He lives in Atlanta.

Visit him online at
www.gillesdeleuzecommittedsuicideandsowilldrphil.com

SEAN KILPATRICK is the author of *fuckscapes*. His writing has appeared in the *Evergreen Review*, *Columbia Poetry Review*, *New York Tyrant*, *Caketrain*, *Dzanc Books Best of the Web 2010*, *30 Under 30*, *Fence*, *The Collagist*, *La Petite Zine*, Spork, Tarpaulin Sky, *The Lifted Brow*, Jacket, *LIT*, 5_Trope, Dark Sky, Juked, elimae, Word Riot, Exquisite Corpse, *3:AM Magazine*, *Bust Down the Door and Eat All the Chickens*, *Cthulhu Sex*, and many other publications. He lives in Michigan.

Visit him online at
www.anorexicchlorinesextoymuseum.blogspot.com

A NOTE FROM LAZY FASCIST

Thank you for purchasing this Lazy Fascist original. Without your continued support, independent publishers like us would cease to exist. I hope you enjoyed *Anatomy Courses* and have an opportunity to discover some of the other wonderful titles in our ever-growing catalog.

If you're just now joining us, we want to welcome you aboard and offer a brief explanation of what we do: Lazy Fascist publishes authors who, through careful exploration of unique linguistic landscapes, create monstrous, unclassifiable fictions. We value explosive language over explosive weapons, but think it's best when we can have our Bruce Willis with our Borges.

We've published everything from minimalist dark comedies to meta-fictional SF, along with historical fiction, fairy tales for adults, and hybrid plays. We seek out books that are emotionally hard-hitting, critically engaging, and exhibit crisp, original prose. These books tend to be difficult to pigeonhole under any one banner, but together they form a complex mosaic of the disenfranchised, the poor, and others who are struggling to survive—and make an impact—in an increasingly bleak world. However, we're not all about doom and gloom. We like to laugh, demand the absurd, and love great storytelling above all else.

If you've been following us for a while, then you know how exciting 2012 will be. Several of last year's releases—*The No Hellos Diet* by Sam Pink, *Of Thimble and Threat: The Life of a Ripper Victim* by Alan M. Clark, and

A Plague of Wolves and Women by Riley Michael Parker—appeared on prominent year's best lists and this year, we'll be publishing even more of today's top authors. Here are a few of the Lazy Fascist titles you can look forward to in 2012:

The Obese by Nick Antosca

Zombie Bake-Off by Stephen Graham Jones

Broken Piano for President by Patrick Wensink

The Devil in Kansas: Three Stories for the Screen
by David Ohle

Colony Collapse by J.A. Tyler

A Pretty Mouth by Molly Tanzer

No One Can Do Anything Worse to You Than You Can
by Sam Pink

I Am Going to Clone Myself Then Kill the Clone and
Eat It
by Sam Pink

The Collected Works of Scott McClanahan Vol. I
by Scott McClanahan

Dodgeball High by Bradley Sands

CPSIA information can be obtained
at www.ICGtesting.com
Printed in the USA
BVHW09s0320030918
526279BV00004B/40/P